W9-BRM-635

STAR WARS
Creatures Big & Small

· GALACTIC BASIC EDITION ·

WRITTEN BY **CALLIOPE GLASS** & **CAITLIN KENNEDY**
ILLUSTRATED BY **KATIE COOK**

DISNEP
LUCASFILM
P R E S S

Los Angeles · New York

Printed in the United States of America

First Edition, October 2019   10 9 8 7 6 5 4 3 2 1

Library of Congress Control Number on file

FAC-034274-19235

ISBN 978-1-368-05082-1

Designed by Leigh Zieske

Visit the official *Star Wars* website at: www.starwars.com.

PORGS

ᴐᗡᴚ7ᗺↀ

Scampering back and forth,
Hopping up and down,
Scrambling south and north,
But always with a frown!

Even when they're happy,
Porgs just look absurd.
And yet, somehow,
They're *still* . . .
The cutest kind of bird.

GORGS

𝓥 ⬠ 𝓥 𝓥 ⬐

Gorgs are like porgs,
Except that they bite.
And they're slimy–
And bug-eyed–
And never take flight.

So, in fact, a gorg
Is *not* like a porg,
I'm really quite sorry to say.
They're the rats of the sea.
I think you'll agree . . .
Porgs beat gorgs any day.

KOWAKIAN MONKEY-LIZARDS

On the far-off planet Kowak,
An impish creature can be found.
And this lizardish, monkeyish rascal
Makes the most annoying sound.

For **monkey-lizards** of Kowak
Don't laugh so much as *shriek*.
It's a one-of-a-kind cackle,
As obnoxious as it is unique.

TOOKAS

ᗐ◌◌⊐⟋⊻

With their big pointy ears
And their fluffy fat tails,
Tookas are hard to ignore.

They're just so cute,
And cuddly to boot.
They're impossible not to adore.

Cat person or not,
Try fighting the thought
Of snuggling one close by your side.

It just can't be done.
Face it: tookas have won.
At least you can say that you tried.

CRYSTAL FOXES

The **crystal foxes** on the planet Crait
Sparkle from head to toe.
These spry little creatures
Are a sight to behold,
With their crystalline bristles like snow.

They're not very cuddly,
And they're not very soft.
They're better to see than to touch.
But when you hear the chime
Of their crystal fur ringing,
You won't mind that they're spiky–
At least, not much.

PUFFER PIGS

A **puffer pig**'s nose is a valuable tool,
But that's not all that makes puffers unique.
When one of these creatures is scared or alarmed,
It balloons to a sizable physique!

These piggies are handy for mining, of course,
But make sure you treat them nicely.
If they're startled or frightened, they'll blow up so fast,
They'll float away, to put it precisely.

CORELLIAN HOUNDS

If you're hoping to find a gentle companion,
If you're shopping for a cuddly cub,
If you're looking for a loyal familiar . . .
Consider looking elsewhere, bub.

Corellian hounds are widely renowned
For hunting and tracking and biting.
But if you *still* really want to adopt one,
At least you've been warned in writing.

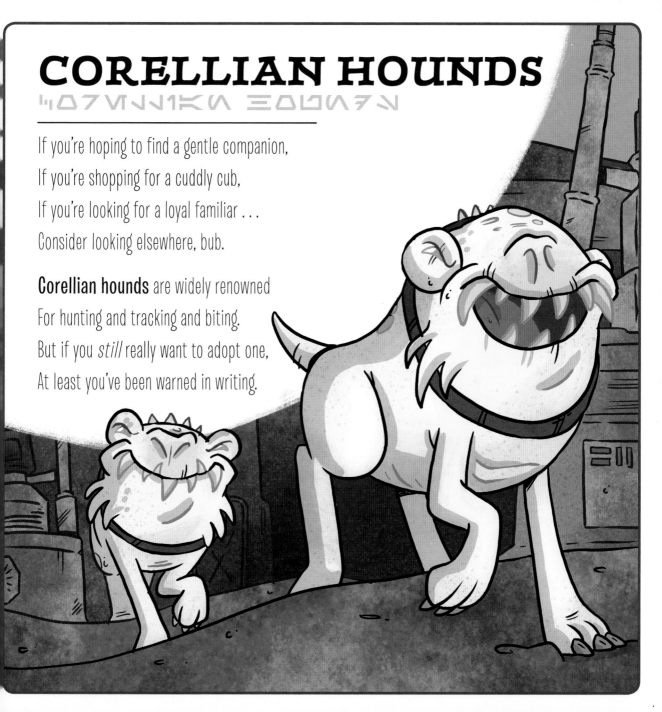

MYNOCKS

Tookas love rats, and porgs like fish,
And humans eat bantha cheese.
But **mynocks** suck power straight out of ships,
Like gigantic bat-winged fleas!

They'll drink from the cables under your hull
And gnaw on your semiconductors.
When it comes to spacefaring vessels and such,
Mynocks are world-class destructors.

So watch out for these flying, fast-feeding foes,
And give a wide berth to their lairs.
Otherwise, you might find yourself stranded
And in desperate need of repairs.

KAADU

A **kaadu** is a weird-looking creature.
Seriously, just take a gander.
It's one part horse
And one part duck.
I hope you don't mind my candor.

A kaadu just looks so darn odd,
Like a tall, two-legged cow.
Then again, people say
It has a keen sense of hearing . . .
So maybe I'll be quiet now.

LOTH-WOLVES

Big and shaggy, gray and white,
Loth-wolves are the pride of the pack.
As long as you're on the side of the light,
Feel free to hop on one's back!

A faster ride you'll never find.
Through hyper tunnels you'll dash.
Loyal and true—and mystical, too—
These wolves are as fast as a flash.

TAUNTAUNS

A **tauntaun** is big.

A tauntaun is tall.

A tauntaun has nothing to fear.

A tauntaun is brave.

A tauntaun is bold.

A tauntaun's the strongest-oh, dear!

WAMPAS

ᗡᛕᐸᑌᛕᐺ

A **wampa** is bigger.

A wampa is taller.

A wampa is vicious and cunning.

A wampa is faster.

A wampa is meaner.

That tauntaun had better start running!

FATHIERS
ᚱᚴᚲᚺᛜᛗᚾᛉ

Graceful, great, and swift,
Fathiers are quite a sight
Along the glittering racetracks
Of the city Canto Bight.

Powerful, strong, and fast,
Yet gentle, majestic, and kind,
These creatures long for freedom,
To no longer be confined.

Fathiers weren't made for sport
But rather the wild, you see—
To run without restraint,
To be at long last free.

DEWBACKS
ᚱᚢᚷᛗᛟᛊᚲᚺᛞᚾ

There are fathiers and reeks and luggabeasts.
There are banthas and tauntauns, too.
But if you're in the desert on Tatooine,
The **dewback** is the ride for you.

The thick choking dust and the harsh desert heat
Will break down the sturdiest creatures,
But with its leathery hide and its wide, webbed feet,
The dewback has all the best features.

RATHTARS

If you took a ball–
About two meters tall–
Gave it teeth to bite
And tentacles to crawl,
And pasted it with
Eyes and warts and all,
Then decided to form
A dozen more–
To make a swarm–
Well, what then?
What would you have?
A pack of **rathtars**
But not a single friend.
And your life would,
No doubt,
Soon be at an end.

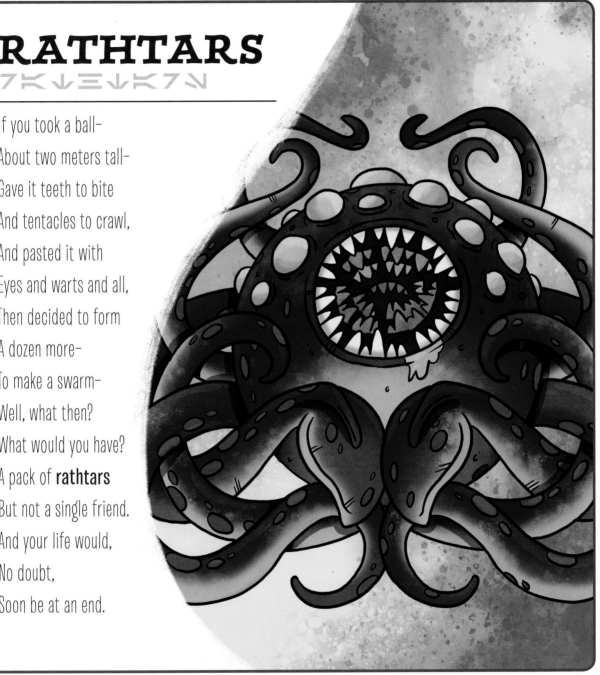

LUGGABEASTS

Stomping through the brush,
Splashing through the bog,
Shuffling through the desert,
Slogging through the fog . . .

Luggabeasts don't tire.
Luggabeasts don't fade.
These cyborg beasts of burden
Are found in every trade.

Be it a pirate, scavenger,
Merchant, or trader,
Everyone uses luggabeasts
(Except Tusken Raiders).

BANTHAS
ƎKИ⅃⅃ƎKИ

Banthas are furry
And warm and good-hearted.
But you'll smell one for parsecs,
Even after you've parted.

That isn't so bad,
Because everyone knows
If you need a bantha,
Just follow your nose.

HAPPABORES

ƎKQQKƎQ7ƔƝ

Happy, happy **happabores**,
Lounging in Jakku's heat.
They never worry about the sun.
In fact, they've got it beat.

What's the secret, happabore?
How do you stay hydrated?
Where do you store (and store and store)
The water you've located?

You see, happabores can drain a pool
With one or two big swallows.
They waddle off, their bellies full,
And leave behind dry hollows.

So if you're thirsty, take a cue
From this happy lumbering lug.
Just make sure you get a drink first,
Before it can *glug, glug, glug.*

VARACTYLS

YK7K⅃⅃∨⅃∨⅃∨

A **varactyl** is a giant reptavian friend
With bright-colored feathers
From head to tail end.

These fast-climbing creatures
Are loyal and tame.
And they only eat plants,
So they won't ever maim.

To ride a varactyl
Is a wild delight.
What are you waiting for?
Hop on, and hold tight!

RANCORS

Rancor, rancor in its lair.
Through the dark, a beady stare.
An oh-so-ugly, lumbering beastie:
Warty, scaly, stinky, greasy.
Rancor, rancor, you're no beauty,
But you'll always do your duty,
Eating all the folks who visit.
It's not a bad life, rancor, is it?

NEXU, REEKS, ACKLAYS

In a dark, dusty chamber,
Waiting for its turn,
A **nexu** prowls and bristles.
Its four red eyes each burn.

Next door to the nexu,
Locked up till the fight,
A **reek** sharpens its horns,
A terrifying sight.

And over there, an **acklay**
Scuttles on six claws,
Clacking its sharp pincers
And chomping its big jaws.

These monsters all are fighters
In the great Geonosian arena–
A place that's even more dangerous
Than the Mos Eisley cantina.

OPEE SEA KILLERS, COLO CLAW FISH, SANDO AQUA MONSTERS

OPEE SEA KILLERS, COLO CLAW FISH, SANDO AQUA MONSTERS

The oceans of Naboo
Are filled with creepy creatures
With tree-sized razor teeth
And other scary features.
Watch out for the **opee**,
Though it's pretty hard to ignore.
If it gets a taste of you,
It just might want some more.
And don't forget the **colo claw**:
It's got more teeth than brains.
But neither of these creatures
Is the top of the food chain.
Because the biggest, meanest baddie
Down deep in the ocean blue
Is the **sando aqua monster**.
Basically, don't swim on Naboo.

SARLACCS

ꓥꓘꓯꓘꓯꓘ (stylized Aurebesh text)

Is a **sarlacc** a worm,
Or land-dwelling squid–
With tentacles that sprawl?
Or maybe a sarlacc is
Some kind of plant,
Waiting for victims to fall?
Nobody knows
Because nobody's managed
To carefully study a sarlacc.
Brainy biologists who stumble across them
Are quickly turned into a snack.
So keep your distance
From a sarlacc.
Don't be ashamed to flee.
The less we know
About these beasts,
The happier we will be.

PURRGIL

ᑌᒍᑐ᜴᜴ᒪᑐ᜴ᐯ

Purrgil are whales that float out in space.
They fly through the airless void.
Everyone loves a purrgil—that is,
Unless your ship gets destroyed.

You try being as big as a purrgil,
Traveling faster than light.
You'll find it isn't so easy
To dodge a spaceship in flight.

But you can't blame the purrgil.
Really, I promise, they hardly mean any harm.
They're gentle giants, beloved behemoths.
Their size is part of their charm.

SPACE SLUGS

You've landed your ship
Down in a cave,
But now you're not feeling
Quite so brave.
The ground is all gooey,
And the walls are all screwy,
And *what* is that gurgling sound?

You've made a mistake.
Leave this place in your wake.
A **space slug**'s belly
Is no place to stick around.

SUMMA-VERMINOTH

Summa-verminoth is a mouthful to say,
But it's better to say than to see,
As these tentacled space-faring monsters
Rarely allow escapees.

So if you're headed to Kessel,
Do yourself a favor:
Don't tarry or dawdle or coast,
Because you could face the menacing maw of this beast,
And then you and your ship would be toast.

porg

gorg

Kowakian
monkey-lizard

tooka

crystal fox

puffer pig

Corellian hound

dewback

rathtar

luggabeast

bantha

nexu

reek

acklay

opee sea killer

sarlacc

purrgil

mynock

kaadu

Loth-wolf

tauntaun

wampa

fathier

happabore

varactyl

rancor

colo claw fish

sando aqua monster

summa-verminoth

space slug

CALLIOPE GLASS
ᚴᚴᚱᚱᛁᚬᚬᚹ ᛂ ᚬᚴᚴᚱᚱ

Calliope Glass is a children's book writer and editor in New York City. Her favorite *Star Wars* character is Mon Mothma. She likes to solve crossword puzzles, read comic books, and sing very loudly.

CAITLIN KENNEDY
ᚴᚴᛁᚱᚱᛁᚬ ᛂᚹᚹᚹᛁᚱᚴ

Caitlin Kennedy lives in San Francisco with her husband, mere miles from the redwoods that inspired the forests of Endor. She has yet to see an Ewok.

KATIE COOK
ᛂᚴᚱᛁᚹ ᚴᛂᛂ

Katie Cook is an illustrator and writer who has been creating work for *Star Wars* professionally for almost a decade, and unprofessionally with crayons since the mid-1980s. She lives in Michigan with her husband, her daughters, and lots of *Star Wars* toys . . . er, collectibles.